WELCOME TO
PASSPORT TO READING
A beginning reader's ticket to a brand-new world!

Every book in this program is designed to build read-along and read-alone skills, level by level, through engaging and enriching stories. As the reader turns each page, he or she will become more confident with new vocabulary, sight words, and comprehension.

These PASSPORT TO READING levels will help you choose the perfect book for every reader.

READING TOGETHER
Read short words in simple sentence structures together to begin a reader's journey.

READING OUT LOUD
Encourage developing readers to sound out words in more complex stories with simple vocabulary.

READING INDEPENDENTLY
Newly independent readers gain confidence reading more complex sentences with higher word counts.

READY TO READ MORE
Readers prepare for chapter books with fewer illustrations and longer paragraphs.

This book features sight words from the educator-supported Dolch Sight Words List. This encourages the reader to recognize commonly used vocabulary words, increasing reading speed and fluency.

For more information, please visit passporttoreadingbooks.com.

Enjoy the journey!

Little, Brown and Company

Hachette Book Group
1290 Avenue of the Americas, New York, NY 10104
Visit us at lb-kids.com

Little, Brown and Company is a division of Hachette Book Group, Inc.
The Little, Brown name and logo are trademarks of Hachette Book Group, Inc.

The publisher is not responsible for websites (or their content) that are not
owned by the publisher.

First Edition: September 2016

ISBN 978-0-316-39464-2

Library of Congress Control Number: 2016946389

10 9 8 7 6 5 4 3 2

CW

Printed in the United States of America

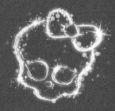

GHOUL POWER

Adapted by Perdita Finn
By Gina Gold
Illustrated by Jessi Sheron

Based on the screenplay by Dana Starfield
and Shane Amsterdam

LITTLE, BROWN AND COMPANY
New York   Boston

Draculaura was a friendly vampire, but she didn't have any friends. She didn't know any other ghouls.

She turned into a bat to fly
with her dad.
She saw a billboard for Tash,
her favorite singer!
Would Draculaura ever go
to a Normie concert?

Draculaura had a vlog
but no one was listening,
except Webby, her pet spider.

Ding dong!

It was the doorbell!

A ghoul had followed them home.

Her name was Frankie Stein.

She wanted a friend too.

The ghouls got to know each other.

"Favorite song?" asked Frankie.

Draculaura smiled.

"'Flawless,' Tash's new hit single."

Draculaura and Frankie wanted
to do normal things.
They even wanted to go to school.
Hey! That was a great idea!
What about a school for monsters?

9

The ghouls searched for other monsters.
Clawdeen Wolf was their first new friend.
Clawdeen was a clawesome werewolf.
She wanted to come to Monster High!

Back at home, Frankie told Draculaura
about the Monster Web.

"Mind blown!" said Draculaura.

Now ghouls all over the world could learn about Monster High from Draculaura's vlog!

"The monsters are coming!" exclaimed Clawdeen.

The next friend the ghouls made
was Cleo de Nile.
"It's been a thousand years
since I had friends!" Cleo told the ghouls.
She couldn't wait to go to Monster High.

Soon after, they made friends
with Lagoona Blue.
"Oy, mates!"
Lagoona Blue surfed to shore.

The ghouls had a creeperific time together in art class.

Skelly was a funny model!

The monsters learned about the human world from Dracula.

Frankie wanted Draculaura to run for school president.

"How about we run together? As a team!" said Draculaura.

"A vote for Frankie and Draculaura is a vote for monsters everywhere!"

Clawdeen and Cleo had a message.
"We have a report of a monster
off the grid.
Her name's Moanica D'Kay."

"Poor Moanica!" said Draculaura.
"Think how excited she'll be
when we show up."
The ghouls were going to rescue her!

Moanica ruled over a graveyard.
She had an army of Zomboyz
who did whatever she wanted.
She didn't want to be rescued.

The Zomboyz attacked the ghouls!

Draculaura turned into a bat!

Clawdeen turned into a wolf!

The ghouls fought back.

They were a team.

Moanica was defeated...but not for long.

Now she wanted to take over Monster High!
"I'm going to run for school president,"
she declared.

"A vote for Frankie and Drac is a vote for kindness!" said Draculaura.
But Moanica wanted to prove that humans were frightened of monsters.

Moanica dared Draculaura to invite
Tash to Monster High!

Draculaura went to find Tash.

But Tash seemed scared of Draculaura.

Draculaura was disappointed.
"Maybe monsters and humans weren't
meant to live together."

But Draculaura's friends had good news.
She and Frankie were elected copresidents.
The monsters believed in her—
not Moanica!

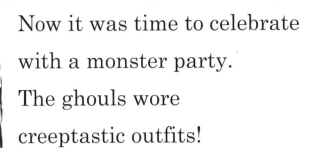

Now it was time to celebrate
with a monster party.
The ghouls wore
creeptastic outfits!

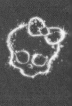

Then Moanica showed up.

She brought someone with her.

It was Tash!

"Let me go, you monsters!"

cried the singer.

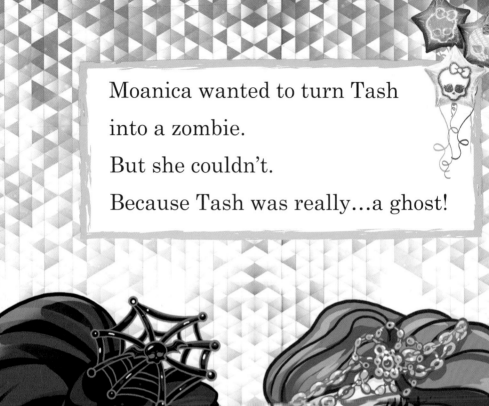

Moanica wanted to turn Tash
into a zombie.

But she couldn't.

Because Tash was really...a ghost!

Tash was a monster too!

She would sing for Monster High!

Draculaura's dreams were coming true.

None of the ghouls would ever be lonely again.
They had one another!
They couldn't wait for their next
adventure at Monster High!